IT TAKES A VILLAGE

BAKERY

Thanks for the support Enjoy the Adventure!

A HEROIC FAIRY TALE

Written by Cindy Flood
Illustrations by Haley Passmore

For Lando,
who is my oxygen

Heartfelt and endless thanks to Randy,
who provided the laptop I used to write this adventure

To my butterfly Dennis,
who is always there for me

Many thanks to my forever friend Lori,
who read the first draft of this
adventure to her wonderful grandchildren,
Hadley and Chase

To Steph, who listens with her whole heart

And to Chrystal, who lights up Olivia and me, always

And
for my brother Terry, thank you for being you

It Takes a Village, A Heroic Fairy Tale
Text copyright © 2021 Cindy Flood

ISBN # : 978-1-7778196-0-6

Printed in Canada, first edition printed November 2021.

Many thanks to the wonderful team of Steve
and Haley of Creative Connex. It is with their
understanding, patience and talent that this
amazing work was realized.

www.creativeconnex.com

Publication assistance and digital printing in Canada by

PageMaster.ca

Hello Everybody!

To help you read this book, here are some hints on how to pronounce the characters' names:

King Landos (Land oos)

Prince Mils (Rhymes with spills or fills)

Caves of Yrret (Why ret)

The Fairies Three:

Ydnic (Yid nick)

Irol (I roll)

Sinned (Sigh ned)

Enjoy the grand adventure!

It was a lazy, hazy day, and the bright yellow sun smiled from far above. A few clouds like bits of fluffy marshmallows dotted the sky. Birds were singing their sweet songs and green, yellow, and blue butterflies fluttered in the warm breeze. They floated above lush green fields where hardworking farmers were tending to their crops.

The breeze carried the butterflies down to the barn, where villagers were milking cows, feeding chickens, and collecting the eggs.

They fluttered towards the village bakery, where the sweet smell of the day's freshly baked bread filled the air. The smell drifted with the butterflies over the rolling hills towards the castle.

Through the castle window and down the hallways they went, gently resting on the arm of King Landos, where he was relaxing in his big comfy royal throne.

As the butterflies rested on the King's arm, he said to his son, Prince Mils, "I will miss that sweet smell of freshly baked bread." The Prince replied, "Miss the smell of the bread? Where are you going, Father?" "Well, I must go to our sister Kingdom, as I am needed there for a royal wedding." "But Father, it is a four-day carriage ride!" "I know my son, but you and the villagers can surely look after our Kingdom while I am away. I will leave in the morning." "All right, Father. I wish you a good trip."

Morning came, but the sun was not as bright. No birds were singing, and the butterflies were nowhere to be seen. Prince Mils feared a storm may be coming and asked his father, "do you think you should still leave on your trip today?" King Landos was packed, his royal carriage was waiting, he knew he must go. He said to his son it would all be fine and to look after the Kingdom. Prince Mils waved to his father as the royal carriage started the long journey.

Hours had passed since the King had left for the journey. Prince Mils wanted to honor the King's wish of looking after the Kingdom, so he mounted his horse and rode into the village. As he was visiting with the farmers and the bakers, a strong, cold wind blew in. Big, beastly clouds hid the sun. The day grew dark. The wind blew even stronger, howling through the village and tearing at the villagers' clothes.

Cracks of thunder snapped. The sky lit up with bright flashes of lightning. Then the rain started. But not just any rain. The Prince and the villagers had never seen a storm like this. The rain quickly flooded the village streets. The farmers' crops washed away and the bakery filled with rainwater. Even the flour needed for the freshly baked bread was soaked and ruined.

"Everyone to the castle!" Prince Mils declared. "The castle is high on the hill and is strong. We will be safe there."

As they made their way to the castle, the villagers asked the Prince if he thought their King would be safe on his journey. The Prince answered, "The King has already travelled far from our Kingdom. Perhaps he is past the storm. Let us hope he is spared from the wind and rain."

The Prince and the villagers settled in for a long, scary night. The castle was high on the hill, and it was dry and safe. But the thunder cracked, the wind howled, and the rain continued to flood the village below. "We need to get some rest," Prince Mils told the villagers. "We will see how our village is tomorrow, after the storm has passed."

Morning came with bright blue skies. The storm had indeed passed. The birds were singing their sweet songs and the butterflies were floating through the breeze. But the land was in ruins.

The villagers looked over their land and said, "Prince Mils, the sister Kingdom is beyond the mountains, and the storm may have spared it. Our Kingdom is small but the sister Kingdom is grand and has many supplies. You must go there and bring King Landos back with supplies or we will surely starve."

"It is a long journey and supplies will be needed before then," replied Prince Mils. "We need a plan." The villagers indeed had a plan, but they would have to reveal a secret so old and well kept that even King Landos or Prince Mils did not know of it.

The secret had been carried down from generation to generation and sworn to secrecy within the village clans. The villagers knew they would have to share the secret with Prince Mils if their Kingdom was to be saved. They told the Prince about Ever Ever Ever Land, where the magic folk lived. Folk that stay in childlike form even though they are hundreds of years old. Among these childlike folk lived The Fairies Three.

It is The Fairies Three that had given Olivia the Dragon a sleeping potion and put her in the Caves of Yrret. Although Olivia had helped villagers in the past, there were some people in the lands that did not like dragons. The Fairies Three knew that hiding her in the Caves of Yrret was the best way to keep her safe.

It is The Fairies Three that can lead the way to the Caves of Yrret and wake Olivia the Dragon from her long sleep.

Two villagers must be chosen to make the journey to Ever Ever Ever Land to call on The Fairies Three. The two villagers and The Fairies Three will make the journey to the Caves of Yrret and wake Olivia.

The rest of the villagers started cleaning and clearing what the storm had left around the Kingdom. They worked long and hard until day turned to night. Prince Mils was pleased with their efforts.

"All of you have done a great deal of work today," he told the villagers. "Now our land is ready for my return from the sister Kingdom with the supplies and seeds. Our two trusted villagers will arrive at sunrise with Olivia the Dragon. We will replant our crops and rebuild our bakery. Now let us all get some rest. I will leave tomorrow for the sister Kingdom."

Morning broke, bringing with it excitement as the Prince and the villagers welcomed back the two brave villagers from their quest. The Prince was indeed pleased the quest was successful. He climbed onto Olivia the Dragon and shouted with joy, "We will return with the King, supplies and seeds!" The villagers cheered and waved as Prince Mils and Olivia flew off on their important mission.

Olivia and Prince Mils flew high over the rolling hills toward the mountains. Beyond the mountains lay the sister Kingdom. They flew all day, and because Olivia the Dragon was no ordinary dragon, they could fly all night too. Olivia was special because her forehead held a magical crystal. It could contact The Fairies Three and fill the night sky with its dazzling light. Just as the sun was setting, they were past the rolling hills and nearing the vast forest at the edge of the mountains.

As night came, Olivia's crystal lit up the dark black sky. The moon was hidden by thick clouds and Prince Mils feared another storm might be coming. The winds started blowing, but Olivia knew she and the Prince had to carry on. Down came the rain! Thunder cracked and lightning sparked all around them, still Olivia flew on. The storm grew stronger, but Olivia flew faster and Prince Mils hung on tighter. As the storm grew more powerful, Olivia was becoming weaker and weaker and her crystal was getting dimmer and dimmer.

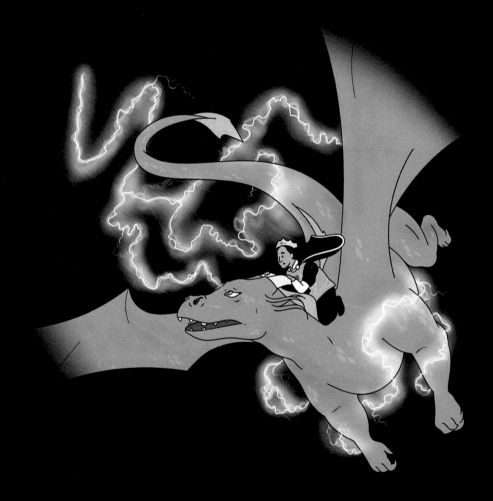

A crack of thunder shook the night sky. A sudden bolt of brilliant lightning hit Olivia! Prince Mils knew they had to seek shelter deep in the forest until the storm passed.

The Prince and Olivia flew down to the forest floor and found a cave opening where they could wait out the storm. Olivia laid down, hurt and sore from the lightning that had struck her. Prince Mils feared she might not be able to continue the journey. Then he remembered what the villagers had said: if Olivia was hurt, he could rub her crystal while calling out the names of The Fairies Three, and they would appear. So, the Prince rubbed Olivia's crystal and spoke the names of The Fairies Three, "Ydnic, Sinned, Irol. Ydnic, Sinned, Irol. Please come now!"

Immediately there was a rumbling in the forest. The wind calmed and a bright light appeared. It was The Fairies Three! They had heard the Prince and come to save Olivia! The Fairies Three were indeed magical and had many potions. They had not only the potion that put Olivia to sleep in the Caves of Yrret hundreds of years ago, but healing potions too. The Fairies Three saw where Olivia had been struck by lightning and conjured up a great healing potion.

As The Fairies Three sprinkled the potion onto Olivia's head, Prince Mils noticed that the mighty storm had passed. The brilliant light of the full moon lit up the mouth of the cave.

Olivia opened her eyes. The Fairies Threes' potion had worked! Her crystal shone brightly and she felt strong and powerful once again. Now the Prince and Olivia could continue their important mission to the sister Kingdom. The Prince thanked The Fairies Three as they left the forest.

The bright full moon and Olivia's magical crystal lit up the night sky and they continued their journey to the sister Kingdom. Olivia flew high and flew strong. They could see the mountains in the far distance, so they pushed on.

After flying through the night and all the next day, the mighty gates of the sister Kingdom appeared. Prince Mils held tight to Olivia as they flew down.

The Royals and King Landos greeted the weary travellers with surprise. "Why are you here, Prince Mils? And who is your magnificent friend?" "This is Olivia the Dragon, and she is my Kingdom's hero. Father, a great storm came over our Kingdom and washed away our crops and bakery.

The Fairies Three woke Olivia the Dragon, and together we flew long and hard to reach you. You must gather as many supplies and seeds as the sister Kingdom can spare and come back with us. We must replant our crops and rebuild our bakery."

The King was saddened by the news but knew the sister Kingdom had much to spare. With the supplies and seeds, his Kingdom would be rebuilt. The Royals of the sister Kingdom were happy to help King Landos with whatever he needed. They gathered the supplies and seeds and rested for the night.

Morning came and Olivia was loaded with the supplies and seeds. The Royals wished King Landos and Prince Mils a safe journey home. Olivia again flew high and flew strong over the mountains and past the vast forest. They flew through the night and Olivia's crystal lit up the dark sky. At sunrise, the long lush rolling hills of their Kingdom appeared.

"Father, we are nearing our Kingdom!" King Landos and Prince Mils could hear the cheers of the villagers welcoming them home. They held tight to Olivia as she flew down to the main Courtyard where they were surrounded by the happy villagers.

"We are glad to be home, but are tired and must rest," said the King. "We will start our work tomorrow and rebuild our land."

The next morning, the King, the Prince, and the villagers were eager to start replanting their crops and rebuilding their bakery. For six days, they worked long and hard. When the sixth day turned to night, King Landos declared, "Soon our Kingdom will be magnificent once again! Tomorrow we shall have a grand carnival in our main Courtyard. All the villagers, Olivia the Dragon, and The Fairies Three will join in the celebrations! Rest now my hard workers, for you have earned it. Tomorrow we will sing and dance!"

The morning sun smiled over the Courtyard where the villagers were busy preparing for the carnival. They looked forward to a grand party to celebrate all their hard work.

There was freshly baked bread, apple pies, and candy apples. There were jesters and face painters and dancers and magicians. It would be a grand day!

King Landos and Prince Mils mounted their horses and rode to the main Courtyard.

"Gather round, my loyal villagers, for I would like to thank each and every one of you. I had no idea when I left for my journey to the sister Kingdom that our Kingdom would fall into ruins from such a nasty storm. It must have been scary! I am sorry I was not here, but your brave plan was a success. The Fairies Three helped by waking Olivia the Dragon. Olivia is indeed a hero! Our Kingdom will forever be grateful. We may all be different, but each and every one of us had something to offer. We have learned a valuable lesson: when we all work together, we are stronger together. It truly does take a village to save a Kingdom! Now let us have a grand time and enjoy the celebrations!"

After a long, fun-filled day of laughing and dancing and singing and eating, night was approaching. The Fairies Three knew the task that lay ahead. Olivia must go back to the Caves of Yrret. The King, the Prince, and all the villagers gathered around Olivia. They thanked her, gave her big hugs, and wished her a long, peaceful sleep.

The Fairies Three and Olivia the Dragon took the journey back to the Caves of Yrret. Once settled, The Fairies Three sprinkled the sleeping potion on Olivia's head and said, "Until you are needed again, sleep well our hero, sleep well."

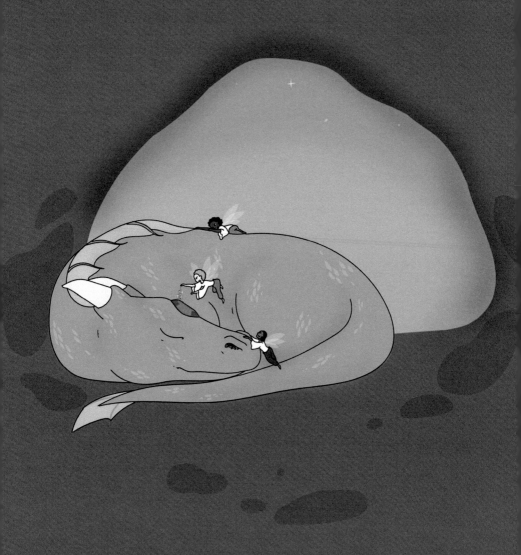

https://pagemasterpublishing.ca/by/cindy-flood/

To order more copies of this book, find books by other
Canadian authors, or make inquiries about publishing
your own book, contact PageMaster at:

PageMaster Publication Services Inc.
11340-120 Street, Edmonton, AB T5G 0W5
books@pagemaster.ca
780-425-9303

catalogue and e-commerce store
PageMasterPublishing.ca/Shop

ABOUT THE AUTHOR

Cindy Flood is a budding new author who calls Edmonton Alberta her home. Since a young girl her love of words and writing short stories grew to the creation of her first children's book. The idea for this first book formed from her fondness for anything dragon-like, (even having an iguana as a beloved pet many years ago).

Wanting to bring a dragon to life in a heroic way, *It Takes A Village* was conceived. She feels strongly that our world needs positive messages to shine through to the next generation. With this first creation being realized, she is working towards the next grand adventure.